W9-CBJ-026

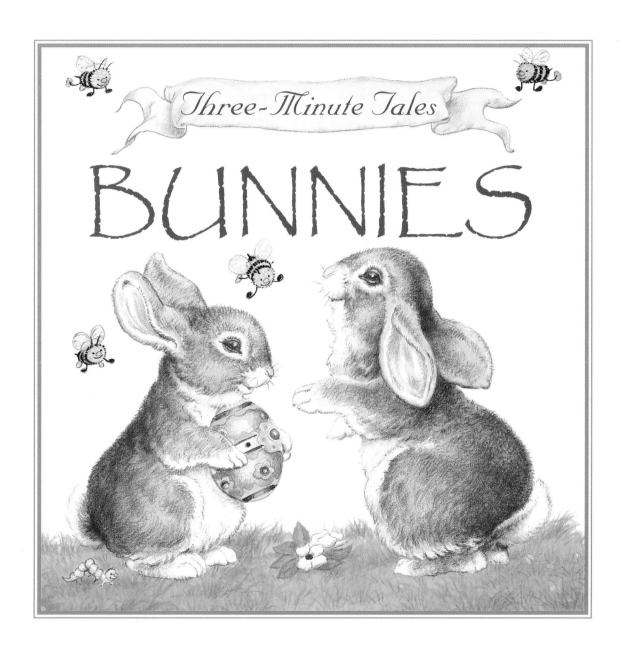

Three-Minute Tales

BUNNIES

p

This is a Parragon Publishing book
This edition published in 2001

Parragon
Queen Street House, 4 Queen Street,
Bath, BA1 1HE, UK

Produced by The Templar Company plc
Pippbrook Mill, London Road, Dorking,
Surrey, RH4 1JE, UK

Designed by Kilnwood Graphics

Copyright © Parragon 2000

Printed and bound in China
ISBN 0 75255 631 2

Three-Minute Tales

BUNNIES

Written by Caroline Repchuk • Illustrated by Mario Capaldi

CONTENTS

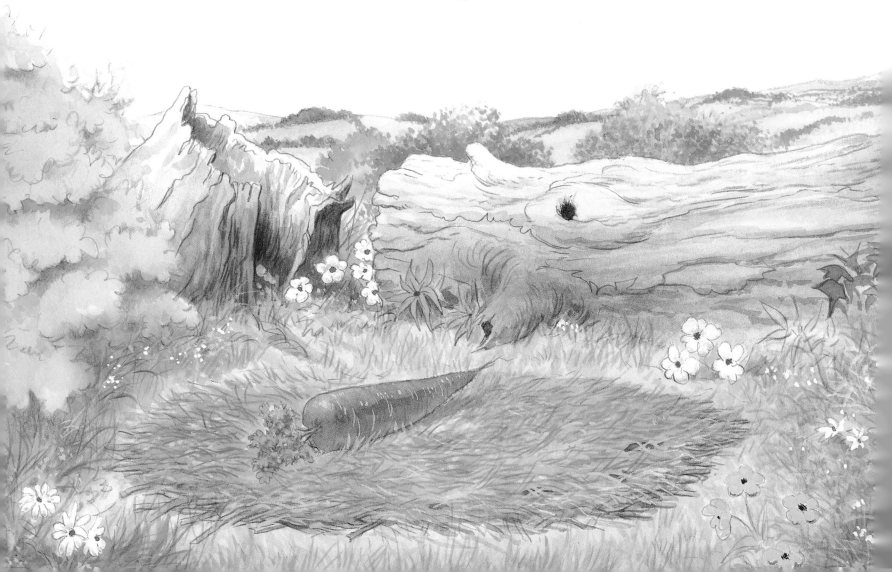

Home Sweet Home

One Bad Bunny

EASTER BUNNIES

It was Easter and the naughty bunnies
had hidden eggs for the animals to find.
How they chuckled when they saw the
farm cat shaking the water from her fur.
She had been searching by the pond
and had fallen in!

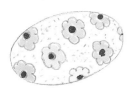

The bunnies giggled as they watched the hens
shooing the pig away from the henhouse.
"They're not in here!" the hens clucked.

Next the little bunnies hurried to the
meadow, where all the sheep were
making a great fuss.

"We've found the Easter eggs!" cried
the sheep, pointing behind a tree.
"Those are toadstools!" laughed the
bunnies. "Keep looking!" By now, the
animals had searched high and low.
"We give up!" said Daisy, the cow.

"Here's a clue," said the bunnies.

"Where do you find eggs?"

"In a nest," answered Mrs Goose.

"And what do you make a nest with?"

asked the bunnies.

"Straw!" said the horse.

"They must be in the haystack!"

The animals rushed to the field and

there, hidden in the haystack, was a

pile of lovely Easter eggs.

What a feast they had!

BUNNY TAILS

Bunnies come in all different colors and sizes. Some have long ears and some have floppy ears. But all bunnies have fluffy tails. All except Alfie, that is. He had no tail at all and his friends teased him badly. "Never mind, dear," said his mommy. "I love you, tail or no tail."

But Alfie did mind and at night he cried himself to sleep. Then one night he dreamt he met a fairy and told her all about his problem. "A little fairy magic will soon

fix that!" said the fairy. She took some dandelion clocks and sewed them together to make a lovely fluffy tail. "Turn around!" she said and fixed it in place in a flash.

Alfie woke with a start. "If only my dream could come true," he thought sadly and looked down at his back. And there, to his astonishment, was a fine fluffy white tail!

"I'm a real bunny at last!" he said proudly, running off to show his new tail to his friends.

HOME SWEET HOME

Bella Bunny looked at the sweet green
grass growing in the meadow on the far side
of the stream. She was tired of eating the
rough grass that grew near her burrow.
"I'm going to cross the stream!" she said to
her brothers and sisters, pointing to a
fallen branch that lay across it.

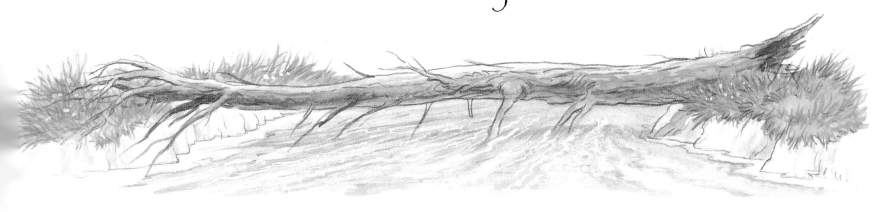

Bella bounced safely across the branch
and was soon eating the sweet, juicy grass
on the other side of the stream.
Her brothers and sisters thought she was

very brave and wondered if they should follow. But just then, they saw a sly fox creeping up behind Bella through the grass! "Look out!" they called.

Bella turned to see the fox just in time!
She leapt back onto the branch, but she
was in such a hurry that she slipped and
fell into the stream. Luckily Becky Beaver
had been watching and she pulled
Bella safely to the other side.
"Home sweet home!" gasped Bella.
And she ran off to join her brothers and
sisters, vowing never to leave home again.

ONE BAD BUNNY

Barney was a very bad bunny. He liked playing tricks on his friends. Barney hid Squirrel's nut store and it took him all day to find it. He put sticky honey on Badger's walking stick and Badger was chased by bees. And he put black paint on Mole's glasses, so poor Mole got even more lost than usual!

"It's time we taught that bad bunny a lesson!" said Badger crossly. So that night, while Barney was sleeping, Mole and Badger dug a big hole. Squirrel climbed up to the treetops and fetched some branches to put

over the hole and they covered it with grass.
They set a big juicy carrot on top, then hid
behind the trees to wait.

The next morning, Barney came bouncing out of his burrow, spotted the juicy carrot and jumped straight into the trap! "Help!" he cried, from the bottom of the hole. The others appeared. "We tricked you!" they laughed. They only let Barney out when he promised to stop playing tricks. And from then on he was a very good bunny indeed.

The End